Adapted by Frank Berrios

A Random House PICTUREBACK® Book

Random House 🏠 New York

randomhousekids.com
ISBN 978-0-7364-3281-8
MANUFACTURED IN CHINA
10 9 8 7 6 5 4 3 2

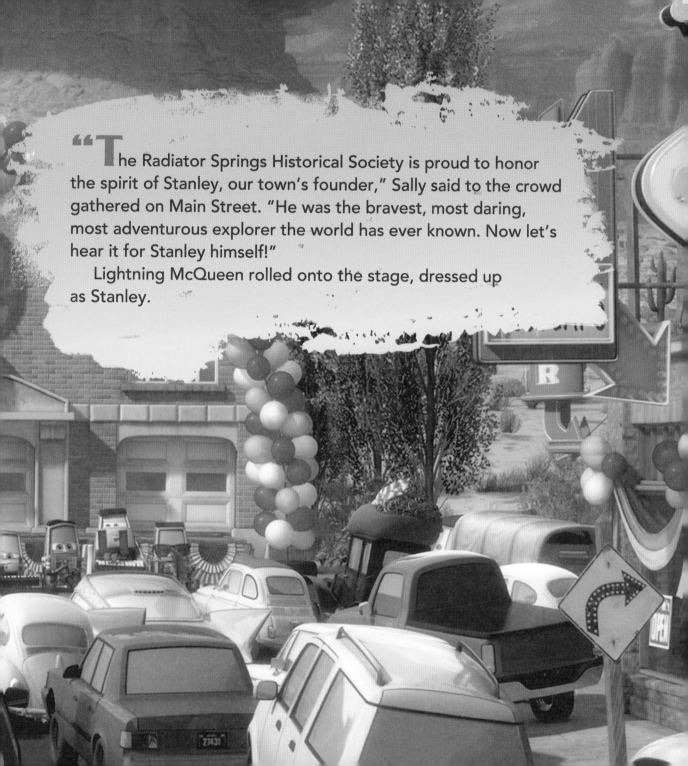

"The Radiator Springs Historical Society is proud to honor the spirit of Stanley, our town's founder," Sally said to the crowd gathered on Main Street. "He was the bravest, most daring, most adventurous explorer the world has ever known. Now let's hear it for Stanley himself!"

Lightning McQueen rolled onto the stage, dressed up as Stanley.

"Well, howdy, friends!" said Lightning, pretending to be Stanley. The crowd chuckled when they saw Lightning's funny costume. "The path I took when I discovered Radiator Springs is full of beauty," Lightning continued. "Let's take a leisurely drive to celebrate the sights."

Suddenly, a group of off-road racers appeared. Their engines roared as they kicked up dust on their way into town. Everyone turned, and the racers came to a screeching halt in the middle of the street.

"Anyone seen Lightning McQueen?" asked Sandy Dunes, the leader of the pack. "We heard he's the fastest car in the West."

"I'm Lightning McQueen," replied the red racer.

"You don't look very fast to me!" Sandy chuckled. It was a challenge!

"Looks like our leisurely drive just turned into a race," Lightning told the crowd. With help from his friends Guido and Luigi, he quickly swapped the Stanley costume for some off-road racing gear!

Sandy and Lightning joined Blue Grit, Shifty Sidewinder, and Idle Threat at the starting line. Before the race could begin, Mater used a map to explain the route the racers would take. But his directions weren't very clear, and the racers quickly became confused.

"So, left at the tractors?" asked Sandy.

"Right!" replied Mater.

"And by right, you mean left," said Lightning.

"Left is right," answered Mater.

"Enough already!" yelled Sandy. He was ready to race!

The cars revved their engines and Sheriff shouted, "Go!" The racers took off down Main Street, burning rubber, then turned onto a dirt road.

"How's our dust taste, city boy?" Sandy teased.

"Not as good as mine!" replied Lightning, pulling ahead. But as the racers approached a fork in the road, they couldn't remember which way to go.

The racers struggled up a very steep hill. When they reached the top, they slammed on their brakes at the edge of a cliff. It was a *long* way down.

"There's no way that Stanley fella could've done this," said Sandy.

"What's the matter? You guys giving up?" asked Lightning, roaring over the top of the hill. He drove straight over the edge!

"After him!" yelled Sandy.

At the bottom of the hill, the racers crashed through a cactus field and into a dark cave.

"Huh! This must be Taillight Caverns," said Sandy.

"Whoa, wait a minute," said Lightning. "Those aren't taillights, they're tail*pipes*!"

Tailpipes jutted out of the ground at odd angles. Without warning, the racers were blasted in the face with exhaust and soot from the pipes!

The soot-covered racers quickly made their way out of the cavern.
"That was *exhausting*," said Sandy.

Next, the racers entered a dark forest just as the sun was setting. "Where are we?" asked Sandy. Before anyone could reply, Lightning rolled over a headlight that was lying on the ground.

The racers followed a trail of broken car parts until they saw the frame of a half-buried car sticking out of the ground! "Aaahhhh!" screamed Lightning and Sandy when they backed into another car.

Everywhere they turned, the racers saw rusting and rotting cars.
Some of the wrecks looked like they were climbing out of graves!
Sandy shivered as he realized they were surrounded!

"I just want to live!" cried Sandy.
Lightning and the other cars took off
screaming, driving fast out of the forest.

The pack was soon zipping back down Main Street. They screeched to a halt at the finish line near the statue of Stanley. The townsfolk wanted to know if the racers had enjoyed Stanley's "leisurely drive."

"Leisurely?" sputtered Sandy. "Your founder was one tough customer!"

The townsfolk smiled when they heard Sandy compliment Stanley. Lightning agreed with him. "The roughest, toughest car in the West," he said proudly.

The off-road racers stared in awe at Stanley's statue. Little did they know, they had gone the wrong way, thanks to silly Mater's confusing directions!